PUFFIN B

Sheltie and

Make frien

Sheltie

The little pony with the big heart

Sheltie is the lovable little Shetland pony with a big personality. His best friend and owner is Emma, and together they have lots of exciting adventures.

Share Sheltie and Emma's adventures in

Peter Clover was born and went to school in London. He was a storyboard artist and illustrator before he began to put words to his pictures. He enjoys painting, travelling, cooking and keeping fit, and lives on the coast in Somerset.

Also by Peter Clover in Puffin

The Sheltie series

Sheltie and the Stray

Peter Clover

PUFFIN BOOKS

For Renée and Alexander

PUFFIN BOOKS

Published by the Penguin Group
Penguin Books Ltd, 27 Wrights Lane, London W8 5TZ, England
Penguin Putnam Inc., 375 Hudson Street, New York, New York 10014, USA
Penguin Books Australia Ltd, Ringwood, Victoria, Australia
Penguin Books Canada Ltd, 10 Alcorn Avenue, Toronto, Ontario, Canada M4V 3B2
Penguin Books (NZ) Ltd, Private Bag 102902, NSMC, Auckland, New Zealand

Penguin Books Ltd, Registered Offices: Harmondsworth, Middlesex, England

First published 1998
1 3 5 7 9 10 8 6 4 2

Created by Working Partners Ltd, London W12 7QY

The moral right of the author has been asserted

Set in 14/20 Palatino

Made and printed in England by Clays Ltd, St Ives plc

British Library Cataloguing in Publication Data
A CIP catalogue record for this book is available from the British Library

ISBN 0–141–30137–6

Chapter One

It was a cold, frosty morning in Little Applewood. Emma was out riding through Bramble Wood on Sheltie, her little Shetland pony.

Emma was on a mission. She was riding Sheltie through the woods behind Horseshoe Pond looking for wildlife. Emma had chosen 'Wildlife and Woodlands' as her special school project and was out riding extra early to see if she could spot anything unusual.

Sheltie was really excited at being out on a ride so early in the morning. His hot breath made little puffs of steam when he blew through his nostrils. And his shaggy mane bounced against his neck as he trampled through a thick carpet of autumn leaves.

Emma was wrapped up like a Christmas parcel in her warm, padded anorak. She pulled back her glove and checked her wristwatch. It was eight o'clock.

'Time to be heading back,' said Emma. 'Nothing much to report today, Sheltie. Not even a squirrel!'

Sheltie rustled his nose into a pile of leaves and gave a loud sneeze.

'Bless you!' said Emma. Then she

2

laughed as Sheltie uncovered a cluster of acorns.

'Thank you, Sheltie,' she said. 'But I've already got lots of acorns.'

Sheltie tossed his head and snorted loudly. Then he began pawing at the ground with his hoof. Sheltie scraped away the covering of dry leaves and this time he pulled out a large conker, still in its prickly overcoat.

'That's a whopper, Sheltie,' laughed Emma. 'I've got conkers too, but none as big as that! It's the size of a tennis ball!'

Emma gave Sheltie a hearty pat on his neck and Sheltie swished his tail. This time the little pony seemed to know that he had found something special. Emma carefully picked up the giant conker and slipped it into her pocket.

As they trotted back through the woods, Emma kept a lookout for foxes, rabbits, hedgehogs, mice and even badgers. Emma was *really* hoping that she might be lucky enough to see a badger even though she knew that mostly they come out at night. She had Dad's camera tucked away in her big zipper pocket.

Then just before they reached the edge of the wood, Sheltie stopped suddenly and flicked up his ears.

'What is it, boy?' asked Emma. Then she heard a twig snap behind her and turned round in the saddle.

Sheltie blew a snort and turned his head too. They both looked, but there was nothing to see. Then Emma heard a rustling sound coming from behind a

4

tree to their left. Sheltie's ears pricked up again and he blew softly.

'Shh, Sheltie!' whispered Emma. 'There's something over there! It could be a fox.' She unzipped her pocket and reached for the camera, then urged Sheltie to walk forward, very slowly.

Sheltie was staring at the spot where the noise was coming from. Emma held the camera ready.

Suddenly there was a loud *bang* from the other side of the woods behind them. It was the sound of a shotgun firing and it made Emma and Sheltie jump.

Emma swung round again to look back in the direction of the shot. Whatever was rustling behind the tree dived for cover into the undergrowth.

'It must have been a rabbit,' said Emma. 'But whatever it was it's gone now, Sheltie! Someone's out there shooting and scared it off.'

As Emma tucked the camera back into her pocket, Sheltie jangled his bit impatiently.

'Come on then, boy. Home!'

Sheltie walked on, and moments later they stepped out of the woods into the brilliant morning sunshine.

They saw a man walking some distance away with a shotgun cocked across his arm. The man was calling out to someone and kicking at the bushes with his boot as though he were looking for something. Emma didn't like the look of him at all.

'Let's stay here for a moment, Sheltie,'

she said, 'and wait for that nasty man to go.' Emma didn't fancy riding past him. She thought he looked very unfriendly. Emma didn't like men with shotguns.

Sheltie shook his head and jangled his reins. Then he stood perfectly still and waited for Emma to give him the command to 'walk on'.

'He was horrible,' Emma told Dad as she helped herself to toast at breakfast. 'A big scruffy man shooting poor little rabbits. I should have taken his photograph and given it to the police.'

'It's best not to think about it,' said Mum. 'People often get permission to shoot rabbits, so the police probably wouldn't be interested.'

'But it's horrible,' said Emma. 'And I'm going to write about it in my school project.'

'That's probably the best thing you can do,' said Mum. 'After all, it's all part of living in the country.'

The next morning, Emma and Sheltie went to the woods again. Emma was hoping to see the same man out shooting so that she could take his photograph for her school project. But he was nowhere to be seen.

Sheltie kept a sharp lookout too, but the woods were empty. Yet as they wandered about, Emma had a strange feeling that she was being watched. Sheltie seemed to sense it too, and kept looking back over his shoulder and blowing funny little snorts.

Every now and again Emma heard movement in the undergrowth. It was as if something was following them but didn't want to be seen.

The rustling seemed to be getting nearer and nearer. Sheltie was taking long sniffs and becoming quite restless.

'It must be some kind of animal,' whispered Emma. 'But why is it following us? And why is it hiding?'

Sheltie listened to Emma's voice and whickered softly. He didn't understand what Emma was saying but he *did* know that something was hiding out there.

Emma slid quietly from the saddle and crouched low on the ground. She peered under the bushes from a distance, to try to see if she could spot anything.

Emma wasn't scared. She knew that foxes and badgers don't attack people. They were more likely to run away if they saw a human. And rabbits and squirrels could sometimes be curious, but Emma had never heard of them following anyone before. As far as Emma knew, there were no dangerous animals living in the woods.

Even so, there was definitely something there and Emma was going to find out exactly what it was.

She smiled happily. 'You stay right here, Sheltie,' she said. Then she began to crawl towards the bushes.

Suddenly something shot out of the bush in front of her. Emma's scream echoed through the woods.

Chapter Two

Emma gasped with surprise as a black and white dog jumped up on her. Sheltie blew a snort and Emma laughed as the little dog began licking her face with its soft pink tongue.

Sheltie pushed his nose forward and nuzzled the dog's head. Then the dog began covering Sheltie's face with kisses too.

Emma tried to hold the dog, but it

wriggled like a worm in her arms.
Suddenly the little dog seemed
frightened and ran away, back into the
woods.

'Where on earth did *that* come
from?' said Emma. 'Did you see where
it went, Sheltie?'

The little pony pawed at the ground

with his hoof and stared through the trees into the woods.

'Do you think we might find it again, boy? Maybe it's lost. Or its owner's in trouble.'

Sheltie's answer was to stomp the ground with his hoofs.

'Come on then, Sheltie. Let's go and take a look.' Emma climbed back into the saddle and walked Sheltie further into the woods.

They searched and searched but they didn't find anything. Emma called out, in case someone needed help: 'Hello! Hello!' But there was no answer.

She called to the dog. Sheltie called too by neighing loudly. But the little dog didn't return.

'Perhaps it lives near by and has just

14

taken itself out for a walk,' said Emma.
'It's probably gone back home now!'

But Sheltie didn't seem to think so. As
they left the woods he became fidgety
and kept swinging his head round to
look back into the trees.

'Another day with no photographs,'
said Emma. 'Maybe we'll be luckier
tomorrow!'

But the next day it was raining and
Emma didn't go out riding at all.

At breakfast, Mum asked Emma,
'Have you been out to feed Sheltie yet?'

'No,' said Emma. 'I thought I would
wait a while until the rain stops!'

Emma's little brother, Joshua, was
playing with a model pony, galloping it
up and down the arm of his high chair.

15

When he heard Sheltie's name he looked up and laughed. 'Sheltie!' he said, and carried on playing.

'So you haven't been out this morning then, Emma?' said Mum. 'It's just that the milk bottle was knocked over outside on the step and I wondered if you knew anything about it.'

In between mouthfuls of cereal, Emma said, 'No I don't, Mum. I haven't been outside at all.'

'And Sheltie hasn't escaped, has he?' Mum asked.

'No. He's standing in the paddock waiting for his breakfast,' said Emma. 'Why?'

'Well, the milk bottle wasn't just knocked over. All the milk had disappeared too!'

'Couldn't it just have got washed away by the rain?' said Dad, looking up from his newspaper.

'Not really,' answered Mum. 'The back step's under cover of the porch canopy. And there would at least be a small puddle of milk or something! No. It looked as though it had been deliberately spilt and then drunk. There wasn't a trace of milk left, except for a few drops inside the bottle.'

'Sometimes small birds peck the tops off milk bottles and drink the cream,' said Dad.

'But I've never known one to tip a bottle over and drink the whole pint,' laughed Mum.

'Maybe it was a great big bird,' said Emma. 'Like an ostrich!'

Mum burst out laughing. 'I don't think there are many ostriches running loose in Little Applewood,' she said. 'And if there were, then I'm sure we would have noticed!'

'Then it's a mystery!' announced Emma. She loved mysteries.

The next day was Saturday and Emma decided to get up extra early and wait for the milk to be delivered. Whoever was stealing the milk, Emma was determined to catch them in the act and take a photograph of them doing it.

That would be an unusual story to write about for her school wildlife project. Emma was certain of it!

Chapter Three

On Saturday morning, as planned, Emma woke to the sound of her alarm clock, which she had set for earlier than usual. *Beep! Beep! Beep!* She sat up in bed and switched it off.

Emma dressed quickly and pulled on an extra jumper. It felt really cold this morning. 'Right!' she said. 'I'm ready.'

Emma grabbed her camera and tiptoed downstairs. It was already light

as she unlocked the back door and
slipped outside. She knew the milkman
would be coming in about five minutes.

Sheltie looked surprised to see Emma
up so early. He blew a loud snort and
came trotting over to the paddock gate
from his field shelter.

'Don't get too excited,' called Emma.
'We're not going anywhere.' She leaned
over the fence and rubbed his neck.

Sheltie pushed his muzzle into Emma's soft jumper and made snuffly pony noises. Then he watched as Emma ran back up the garden to the tack room. Sheltie wondered what she was up to!

He watched Emma open the tack-room door and slip inside. She left the door ajar and poked her head round the side. Emma was hiding.

Sheltie could still see her and whinnied excitedly. He thought this was some kind of new game. But Emma didn't come out. She stayed in her hiding place and waited.

A few minutes later the milkman arrived. He rolled up in his little white van, then walked up the path to deliver two pints of milk. This morning he brought a loaf of bread too.

Emma and Sheltie watched as the milkman left the milk bottles and bread on the back doorstep. Then he strolled back down the path, whistling to himself.

'Good morning, Sheltie,' he called out, and waved to the little Shetland pony. Sheltie answered by blowing a loud raspberry. Emma giggled from her hiding place. The milkman hadn't seen her.

Emma got ready with her camera.

'Come on, ostrich, or whatever you are. I'm waiting!' Emma could see the doorstep quite clearly from the tack room and was near enough to get a good shot with her camera.

Suddenly Sheltie started playing up. He was blowing hard and snorting and stomping his feet on the grass. Sheltie had seen something.

He lowered his head and watched a small shape go slinking by alongside the garden hedge. Something hairy. Something black and white.

Emma saw it too as it slipped through a gap and padded up the garden path towards the back door.

It wasn't anything strange like an ostrich. Emma had known it wouldn't be really. It was the little dog they had met in the woods!

Emma watched with her camera poised as it found the loaf of bread and began to tear hungrily at the cellophane wrapper.

The poor thing must be starving, thought Emma. She crouched still, and watched the dog eat the slices of bread. It wolfed down half the loaf before it looked up, licking its lips. Then it pushed over a milk bottle, used its teeth to pull off the thin silver top and lapped up the spilt milk.

Click! Whirr! Emma took a photograph. She had solved the mystery and caught the culprit on film.

The little dog was startled by the sudden noise and pricked up its floppy ears. Emma came out of hiding to try and make friends. But the little dog took fright and ran away, leaving the empty bottle and the half-eaten loaf behind.

Emma watched as the dog took off down the path, through the hedge and away up the lane.

Sheltie watched it too and whinnied

as if to say, 'Come back, we won't hurt
you!' But the dog had gone.

Emma ran back inside the cottage to
tell Mum and Dad. She bounded up the
stairs and burst into her parents'
bedroom. Then she bounced on to their

bed and woke them both up with a start.

'It's a dog!' she cried. 'A little black and white dog. I saw it drink the milk and eat our bread.'

Mum rubbed the sleep from her eyes.

'What *are* you talking about, Emma?' she said.

Dad moaned and pulled the covers up over his head.

'The milk thief!' exclaimed Emma. 'It's a dog. And it was starving! It ate the bread and drank the milk and I've got a photo to prove it!'

Mum made Emma explain exactly what had happened. By now, Joshua was awake. He heard all the talking and tottered in to the bedroom to see what was going on. Mum lifted him up on to

26

the bed and he snuggled down between his parents.

With all the excitement, Mum was wide awake. She and Emma got up and left Dad and Joshua to doze.

Downstairs, while Mum made some tea, Emma told how she had seen the little dog two days earlier in the woods.

'It must belong to someone,' said Mum.

'But what if it doesn't?' said Emma. 'What if it's lost or it's been thrown out of its home and is living wild? It's such a lovely little dog. It must be so lonely living out in the woods all on its own!'

'Did it have a collar?' asked Mum.

'I don't know,' answered Emma. 'I didn't see one.'

'Well, perhaps after breakfast you can take Sheltie out into the woods to look for it. If it's a stray, we must try and catch it. We can't have a dog living wild in Little Applewood. It might start bothering Mr Brown's sheep.'

'Oh! I'm sure it wouldn't harm any

sheep,' said Emma. 'It's such a nice, friendly dog. It must have followed me and Sheltie the other morning and seen where we live. It's just hungry and probably scared and lonely too!'

'Well, if you *do* see it again, don't touch it in case it bites,' said Mum, worried.

'But it doesn't,' interrupted Emma. 'It licks and licks and licks. It's really friendly. Honest!'

'Emma!' Mum said sternly. She gave Emma a 'do as you're told' look.

'All right. If I find it, I'll come back and tell you. Or I could get it to follow me home!' she added brightly.

'I'll give you a packet of biscuits then, to take with you in case you do see it again,' said Mum. 'Perhaps it would be best if you *could* get it to follow you home. Then we can decide what to do with it.'

'We could keep it!' said Emma. 'It's such a lovely little dog.'

'I don't know about that, Emma,' said Mum. 'But we could try and find it a nice home. Now help me upstairs with this tea.'

Mum climbed back into bed with Dad and Joshua. But Emma was wide awake. She couldn't wait for breakfast time so she helped herself to cereal in the kitchen. Then she took the biscuits Mum had left out for her and stuffed them into her anorak pocket.

'I'm taking Sheltie over to Sally's,' Emma called up the stairs. 'Then we'll ride through the woods to look for

Scamp.' Scamp was the name Emma had already given the stray dog. Emma thought it looked like a cheeky little scamp.

'OK,' answered Mum. 'But be back for lunch. And remember, Emma, if you *do* find the dog, don't touch him!'

Chapter Four

Sally was Emma's best friend. She had a pony of her own as well. He was called Minnow. Sheltie and Minnow were friends too. Sally lived in Fox Hall Manor, just a short ride away.

It was still early when Emma and Sheltie trotted through the big iron gates of the manor. But Sally was already up and tending to Minnow in his stable at the back of the house.

'Hello, Sally,' called Emma. Sheltie
blew a good-morning snort, and
Minnow answered with a soft whicker.

'You're an early bird!' said Sally. 'It's
only eight o'clock.'

'We're on pony patrol this morning,'
said Emma cheerfully. 'There's a stray
dog living in Bramble Wood and we've
got to find it!'

'A stray dog!' echoed Sally.

Emma told Sally all about Scamp while she tacked up Minnow.

'It's no more than a puppy really,' said Emma, 'and it's so cute and cuddly. If we find it, I'm going to tempt it back to the cottage with some biscuits.' Emma patted her jacket pocket.

When Sheltie heard the biscuit packet rustling, his ears pricked up.

'They're not for you, greedy,' laughed Emma.

Sheltie lowered his head and whickered sulkily.

'Well, maybe one then,' added Emma. 'But not yet. You have to help us find Scamp first!'

Sheltie pricked up his ears again and began prancing on the spot.

'Come on then,' said Sally. 'Let's get going!'

They set off at a steady walk until they reached Mr Brown's meadow. Then they stretched their ponies and cantered across the open field to the edge of the woods.

'Where did you first see Scamp?' asked Sally.

'In the woods up on the old bridle path,' said Emma. 'The one that leads out to the downs. I thought it would be a good idea if we went there first.'

Sheltie and Minnow walked the path side by side, blowing puffs of steam and rustling their hoofs through drifts of fallen leaves.

'The woods always look different when the leaves come down,' said Sally.

'You can see much further through the trees. Look, you can even see that man all the way over there!'

Emma looked across to where Sally was pointing. In the distance, some way off, walking through the trees, was a man with a shotgun cocked across his arm.

Emma recognized him straight away. It was the same man she had seen three days earlier.

Emma didn't fancy riding anywhere near him, so she said to Sally, 'Why don't we go up to the back wood? We never ride up there.'

'It's worth a look,' said Sally. 'There's no sign of a dog anywhere round here, is there?'

'Maybe Sheltie can help us find it,'

said Emma. She leaned forward across Sheltie's neck and whispered in his ear. 'Can you help us find Scamp, Sheltie?' Then she rustled the biscuits.

Sheltie couldn't understand *exactly* what Emma was saying, but he seemed to know that they were looking for something. And maybe there was a titbit for him at the end of it!

Sheltie raised his nose in the air and took a long, deep sniff. Then he blew a sharp snort which made Minnow jump.

They searched the back wood, but found nothing until Sheltie led them down into a gully and suddenly stopped by an old drainpipe. The concrete pipe was almost one metre across and stuck out of a steep bank.

Sheltie pawed at the ground with his hoof, then lowered his head slightly to peer inside the drainpipe.

'Sheltie's found something!' exclaimed Emma.

Sheltie blew a snort of triumph which was answered with a soft bark.

'Did you hear that?' said Emma. Sally nodded. Emma slid from her saddle.

Sheltie was trying to push his head right inside the drainpipe for a better look.

'Come away, Sheltie.' Emma coaxed her little pony away from the drainpipe, then crouched down herself to peer inside.

No sooner had Emma knelt in front of the opening than the little dog

jumped out at her. It covered her face
with kisses. And no matter how hard
Emma tried not to break her promise to
Mum, she couldn't help it. Emma threw
her arms around Scamp and gave the
little dog the biggest cuddle it had ever
had.

Sally dismounted too and fussed and petted the cute stray.

Emma opened the packet of biscuits and watched in amazement as Scamp wolfed down the lot.

'Save one for Sheltie,' said Sally.

Emma grinned. 'I already have.' She thrust her hand into her pocket and produced four biscuits.

'Two for Sheltie,' she said, 'and two for Minnow.'

Scamp looked up and watched Sheltie and Minnow gobble down their treats. Then he looked up at Emma with big, cute eyes as if to say, 'Are there any more?'

'Come on, Scamp,' said Emma. 'The plan is that you're supposed to follow us back to the cottage.'

Scamp wagged his tail. Then he stood up on his hind legs and licked the crumbs from Sheltie's nose.

'I think Scamp will follow you two anywhere,' said Sally.

Chapter Five

From the cottage gate, Mum watched
Emma and Sheltie lead the little stray
dog up the lane. Sally and Minnow rode
a little way behind them.

Scamp looked nervous, but he seemed
happy to follow at Sheltie's heels as they
trotted along.

Joshua stood with Mum and pointed
through the gate.

'Woof, woof,' he said.

'Yes, woof, woof,' said Mum. 'It's a little dog, but we mustn't scare him, Joshua. We've got to be very quiet.'

Joshua put his finger to his lips and said, 'Shh!'

Then they watched as Scamp followed Sheltie up the path to the paddock.

Mum came through the garden gate to greet Scamp. And Joshua stood behind her peering between her legs.

The little dog looked at them both. Then he looked back at Sally and Minnow. Finally he looked at Emma and Sheltie, then gave a little whine before he ran off as fast as his legs would carry him.

Everyone watched in amazement as the little dog shot back up the lane like a rocket.

Emma was so disappointed.

'Oh no!' she wailed. 'He followed us
all the way from the woods and now
he's run off!'

'He probably got frightened,' said
Mum. 'Seeing everybody at once must
have spooked him.'

'Shall we go and see if we can find him again?' said Sally.

Mum thought about it for a moment then said, 'It's probably best to just leave it for now. The dog knows where we are. We'll leave some food and water out and see what happens.'

Sally glanced at her wristwatch.

'I'd better be going,' she announced. 'Mum's taking me into town after lunch to buy new shoes.'

Emma pulled a face.

'I know!' said Sally. 'But I've got to go.'

'I'll phone you tomorrow,' said Emma, and waved as Sally took Minnow off at a fast walk.

After Sally had gone, Emma turned to Mum.

'Do you think Scamp will come back?'
she asked.

'He might,' said Mum. 'We'll go into
the village after lunch and buy some
dog food. Something nice and tasty to
tempt a hungry stray.'

That night, before they went to bed,
Mum left a bowl of dog food and a bowl
of water on the back step.

'I hope Scamp finds his way back,'
said Emma.

Mum brushed the hair out of Emma's
eyes and pulled the bedcovers up,
tucking her in nice and warm.

'Let's see what tomorrow brings,' said
Mum.

The next morning, Emma woke to the

sound of the church bells ringing from
the village.

She sat up in bed and counted the
chimes.

'Eight!' There were eight chimes.
Emma threw back the bedclothes and
grabbed her warm dressing gown. She
made her bed, washed and then dressed
before she hurried downstairs.

When Emma unlocked the back
door and peered out on to the step, a
contented smile swept across her
face.

The two bowls were empty. Scamp
must have come for the food and water.

Emma looked around, but there was
no sign of the little dog. She glanced
down to the paddock. There was no sign
of Sheltie either.

Suddenly Emma was concerned. Sheltie was *always* waiting for her at the paddock gate. But this morning he wasn't there. Where *was* he?

Chapter Six

Emma climbed the paddock fence and hurried across to Sheltie's field shelter. As she peered inside, Emma let out a sigh of relief. Sheltie was lying down on the straw. And there, snuggled between his forelegs, was Scamp, the little stray dog, curled up fast asleep.

Sheltie whickered softly. It was as though the little pony didn't want to wake his new friend. Emma looked

down at her Shetland pony and the little
lost stray.

'Don't worry, Scamp,' whispered
Emma. 'We'll take care of you.'

The little dog opened one lazy eye
and gazed up at Emma. Emma half
expected Scamp to run off again as he

had before. But he didn't. He just closed his eyes and gave a contented grunt. Then he went back to sleep.

Emma ran all the way back to the cottage. Mum and Dad were both in the kitchen laying the table with cups and breakfast plates.

'Come quickly,' said Emma. 'It's Scamp! He's in the shelter curled up asleep with Sheltie. He came back all on his own!'

Dad acted quickly. 'You stay here with Joshua,' he said to Mum. 'I'll use one of my old ties to make a lead. Come on, Emma.' Soon they were off, hurrying down to the paddock.

Emma and Dad poked their heads slowly round the shelter wall and peered inside. Sheltie was still lying on the straw, with Scamp fast asleep between his forelegs.

When Sheltie saw Emma he whickered softly again.

'Shh, Sheltie!' said Dad. He didn't want the little dog to wake up. But it was too late. Suddenly Scamp sat upright and gave a little woof.

Emma crouched down and stretched out her arm towards him. Scamp wagged his tail and licked the back of Emma's hand with his warm, smooth tongue.

'Here,' whispered Dad. 'Slip this tie over his head.'

Scamp sat quite still and made no fuss at all as Emma slipped the makeshift lead around his neck.

Sheltie blew a snort of triumph and

jiggled to his feet. Then he shook out his mane and showered Scamp with straw.

Emma stroked the little dog and Dad made friends with him too. Then they led Scamp up to the cottage to a nice warm kitchen and a bowl of dog biscuits.

'He *must* belong to someone,' said Mum as she handed Joshua a piece of toast spread with honey.

'Nice doggy,' said Joshua. And he threw the toast on to the floor in front of Scamp. Emma giggled as the little dog wolfed it down.

'No, Joshua,' said Mum. 'You mustn't do that!' Then she buttered another piece of toast for Emma's little brother before turning her attention back to Scamp.

'He must belong to someone,' she said again. 'We'll have to ask around. Will you take Sheltie and ride up to Marjorie Wallace's, Emma? She might know if anyone's lost a dog.'

'That's a good idea,' agreed Emma. 'I'll get Sally and Minnow to come too! We can call at all the houses and cottages on the way. If Scamp's gone missing from his home then *someone* must know him!'

Later that morning, Emma and Sally rode all over Little Applewood. The day was bright and sunny, but there was a chilly breeze in the air.

Sheltie and Minnow trotted along happily side by side. Every now and again they came across a deep drift of autumn leaves. Then Sheltie would rustle through them, lifting his hoofs high and trampling as many leaves as he could.

'Sheltie's so funny,' laughed Sally. 'He's always full of mischief, isn't he?'

'That's just how I like him,' said Emma, grinning.

They rode on, up to the barrow and Marjorie Wallace's place. Marjorie had nine cats and looked after all kinds of rescued animals. She hadn't heard of anyone who had *lost* a dog, but she knew of someone who was missing one.

'It's such a shame,' began Marjorie. 'Poor old Fred Berry. He had a dog called Jasper who died last week of old age. Poor Fred is heartbroken, he misses that dog so much.'

Emma felt really sad for Fred. She
tried to imagine what it would feel like
if anything happened to Sheltie!

'If I hear of anyone who has lost a
dog though, I'll let you know,' said
Marjorie.

Emma and Sally rode away. And at

every house and cottage they called at, it was the same. No one had heard of anyone who had lost a dog.

Back at the cottage, Mum decided that it would be a good idea to put a notice in the post-office window first thing Monday morning.

Emma knew that it was the right thing to do. But secretly she still wished that she could keep Scamp for herself.

By lunchtime the next day, Mum's notice was in the post-office window. Emma saw it on her way home from school. It read:

FOUND
Young, black and white, long-haired dog.
Very friendly. Rescued from Bramble Wood.
Contact . . .

Then it gave the address and telephone number of the cottage.

'Has anyone called about Scamp?' asked Emma.

'It's early days yet,' said Mum. 'The notice only went up this afternoon.'

The little dog was curled up warm and cosy in a cardboard box next to the kitchen stove. When he heard Emma come in, he bounded across the floor.

'Come on, Scamp,' Emma said. 'I'll take you for a nice walk before it gets dark.'

Mum had borrowed a proper collar and lead from a friend in the village. Scamp's tail thumped the floor as Emma slipped it on.

Emma tied Scamp outside while she fitted Sheltie's head collar and lead rein.

Then she took both of them for a stroll
before tea.

On the way they bumped into Fred
Berry. Fred used to exercise Jasper every
day at that time. He looked sad and
lonely without his little friend.

'Hello, Emma. Hello,
Sheltie,' he said. 'And
who's this? What a
smashing dog! Where on
earth did you find *him*?'

Emma told Fred Berry
all about Scamp.

'Well, I hope you find
his owner soon,' he
said. 'It's an
awful thing when
you lose an
animal.'

Emma knew that Fred was missing Jasper. But she still didn't really want to find Scamp's owner. Emma kept hoping that she would be able to keep him.

Sheltie liked Scamp too! The whole time as they walked along, Sheltie kept nuzzling the little dog's head and making friendly whickers.

'If no one comes forward,' Emma said to Scamp, 'then we'll *have* to keep you!'

But when Emma got back to the cottage she found that Mum had other plans.

Chapter Seven

'If we don't hear from anyone by the end of the week,' said Mum, 'perhaps we should put an advert in the local paper.'

Oh no, thought Emma. That meant more people would know about Scamp. And more people meant less chance of Scamp staying.

By Thursday, when Emma got home from school, there were still no callers at the cottage. Scamp had settled in nicely and Emma knew that it was going to be really hard to give him up.

'I put a "lost" notice in the *County Gazette* today,' said Mum. 'It should be in the paper tomorrow, so we might hear something from Scamp's owner over the weekend.'

Emma didn't want to hear anything from Scamp's owner at *any* time. For almost a whole week she had been able to pretend that Scamp belonged to her.

Of course Emma knew it was right to try and find Scamp's owner. But she had grown so fond of the little dog, and so had Sheltie.

Over the last two days, Emma had taught Scamp to walk alongside Sheltie on a long lead rein. And Sheltie had seemed to love having the little dog padding along next to him as they walked the lanes.

Scamp jumped up at Emma and cocked his head to one side. Emma scratched his ears and said, 'Don't worry, boy. Maybe no one will answer the advert. Then you can live here for ever!'

Mum pretended she didn't hear Emma, but gave Dad a funny look and raised one eyebrow.

'I'll take Scamp out for a walk with Sheltie before tea,' Emma announced. She dashed upstairs to change out of her school clothes, then clipped the long lead on to Scamp's collar and rushed down the garden path.

When Sheltie saw Emma and Scamp

coming he did a mad dash around the paddock, kicking his heels and snorting loudly.

Emma tied Scamp to the fence while she tacked up Sheltie. The little dog was happy to scamper and roll among the leaves while he waited.

Then Emma unlocked the gate and mounted Sheltie. She took hold of Scamp's long lead and they had a nice long walk up the lane and across Mr Brown's meadow to Horseshoe Pond and back.

Later, when they were all settled at the kitchen table having their tea, Mum had a talk with Emma.

'I know it's going to be hard,' said Mum, 'but if Scamp's owner *does* turn up, we'll have to let him go.'

Emma looked down at her plate and poked at her sausages with her fork.

'But what if nobody *does* turn up to claim Scamp?' she asked. 'Can we keep him?'

Mum looked across at Dad. Then Dad spoke.

'Well, Emma,' he began. 'Keeping a dog is a huge responsibility. I'm working all week and Mum is busy looking after Joshua and helping out at the handicraft shop. And you're at school all day. I don't know if we *can* look after a dog as well!'

Suddenly, Emma felt very sad. 'But he needs a good home,' she said.

'Oh, we'll make certain he finds a good home,' said Mum, 'but it might not be here with us.'

Scamp cocked his head to one side
as though he were listening to every
word.

'Sheltie could look after him when
there's no one here,' she suggested.

'I don't think so, Emma,' said Dad
kindly. 'It wouldn't be fair to Scamp. He
needs someone to look after him all day
long. Like ponies, dogs *can* be a
handful.'

Emma finished her tea in silence.

On Saturday morning, Emma took
Sheltie and Scamp out again for a walk.

But this time, when they came home,
there was a car parked outside the
cottage. One of the car doors was open
and a man was standing there talking to
Dad.

Emma recognized the man at once and felt a twinge of panic. It was the same man she had seen in the woods, carrying a shotgun.

Scamp recognized the man too and began to whine and pull on his lead in alarm.

Emma quickly turned Sheltie out into the paddock and held on tightly to Scamp. The little dog was fretting and squirming to free himself of his collar.

Emma stood a little way off and listened to what the man was saying. He looked across at Emma and Scamp.

'There he is. There's my dog!' the man said in a very loud voice. 'I saw the advert in the papers this morning and came over as soon as I could.'

Emma's heart missed a beat. This man

couldn't possibly be Scamp's owner, she thought. But somehow she knew that it was.

'I live in Rilport, but I was over here last week with the dog and he ran off. I've been looking everywhere for him ever since.'

It sounded horribly true. Emma didn't want to believe it but the man had come to take Scamp away.

Dad stood talking with the man, checking over his story and asking questions. And all the time Scamp tried to hide himself behind Emma's legs. The poor dog was trembling from head to tail.

Then the man produced a piece of paper showing that he had paid twenty pounds for Scamp at a farm.

'That's my dog,' said the man flatly.
'Now hand him over.'

It was hopeless; there was nothing
they could do.

'How do you know he's your dog?'
asked Emma. 'You haven't even looked

at him properly. There are probably hundreds of black and white dogs around just like this one!'

'But I've just told you. I lost him in the woods up there. And that's where you found him. Anyway, I'd recognize him anywhere!' The man was beginning to sound really angry.

Dad didn't like his tone of voice. And judging by the way the dog was behaving, neither did Scamp. But there was nothing Dad could do.

'I'm afraid we'll have to give Scamp back, Emma,' said Dad gently. 'Why don't you carry him over to the car and say goodbye?'

Emma didn't want to, but she scooped Scamp up in her arms and carried him across to the waiting car.

Then Emma did something very risky.
As she put Scamp down on the car seat
she deliberately unclipped the dog's
lead.

Scamp seemed to know exactly what
was happening. As soon as the lead
came free he jumped from the car and
bounded away, running as fast as his
legs would carry him. Emma watched

Scamp dash through a gap in the hedge and scoot across Sheltie's paddock.

When he got to the other side he squeezed through the fence posts and disappeared.

'You stupid girl,' yelled the man. 'You did that on purpose!'

But Emma didn't care. Dad half grinned and said it was obviously an accident. The man's faced turned bright red and he stormed off back to his car. Emma ran indoors. She thought she was in big trouble.

Emma peered through the kitchen window and saw Dad outside talking to the man. Then the man drove away and Dad walked back to the cottage.

I'm for it now! thought Emma.

Chapter Eight

'What an unpleasant man!' said Dad as he stepped into the kitchen. Emma was expecting to be told off, but Dad just smiled. 'Don't worry, Emma,' he said. 'I don't think that man really wanted Scamp back anyway. He'd rather have a mean, rough dog. What you did was very naughty. But I don't blame you. I've given the man the twenty pounds he paid for Scamp,

73

and he's gone for good, I promise
you!'

Emma's face lit up.

'Oh, Dad! Does that mean we can
keep him?' she asked.

'Well, not exactly,' said Dad. 'But at
least Scamp won't be going to live with
someone who doesn't really want him.
Now, why don't you take Sheltie and go
and see if you can find Scamp? Let's just
hope he hasn't gone too far.'

Emma didn't need to be told twice.
She ran to the paddock, mounted Sheltie
and took off at a fast trot to find the little
dog.

Emma searched everywhere for
Scamp. She rode through the woods
calling his name but she couldn't see
him anywhere.

'Where could he have got to?' said
Emma.

Sheltie blew a snort and pawed at the
ground. He tossed his head and looked
around. Sheltie was searching for Scamp
too!

'I bet *you* know where he's hiding,
don't you, boy?' said Emma.

Sheltie lifted his head and sniffed the
cold, frosty air.

'Go on then,' Emma urged. 'Find
Scamp!'

Emma squeezed Sheltie's sides with
her legs and loosened his reins. This was
Emma's signal to let Sheltie go where he
wanted.

The little Shetland took off immediately.
He snorted and sniffed at the air as he
hurriedly walked the bridle path.

Then, suddenly, Sheltie changed direction and turned to head for the back wood.

Sheltie quickened his pace and bounced along, trampling through the leaves.

Once in the back wood, Sheltie made his way to the gully where they had first found Scamp. He stopped at the drainpipe and Emma jumped down from the saddle.

'Well done, Sheltie,' she said, and patted his neck.

Then, as Emma crouched to peer inside, Sheltie blew a snort and Emma heard a sad whine coming from far back inside the concrete pipe.

'Scamp!' called Emma, in no more than a hushed whisper. 'Come out, boy.

You're safe now. Here, Scamp! Here, boy!'

The little dog was definitely inside. Emma could hear him whimpering quite clearly. But Scamp was terrified and wouldn't come out.

'Looks like I'll just have to go in and get him, Sheltie,' said Emma, and she began to crawl inside.

As soon as Emma entered the pipe she felt it move slightly under her weight. Emma stopped for a moment. Cautiously she rocked gently from side to side on her hands and knees. The pipe seemed solid enough.

Emma crept forward, whispering, 'Here, boy. It's me, Emma. Don't be scared. I'm coming to get you!'

As she crawled forward the pipe moved again. Only a little bit, but it seemed to dip in front of her.

Emma could see Scamp now, hiding in the gloom only metres ahead of her. She could also see why Scamp hadn't gone any further. Behind him the pipe had collapsed and was blocked and choked with tree roots. It must have been like that for ages, thought Emma.

She crawled forward and reached out with her hand. She could almost touch Scamp now.

Just a little further and Emma felt his warm, soft tongue licking her hand. Then he came forward and Emma gave him a hug.

She took hold of Scamp's collar and turned round in the pipe ready to clip on his long lead to help the little dog out. Emma could see Sheltie at the end of the dark tunnel, peering in.

'We're coming, Sheltie,' she called. 'I've got him!'

But just then, the pipe moved, and before Emma could crawl out, the

entrance collapsed. A big piece of
concrete came down with a crash and
blocked her exit.

Emma screamed. Sheltie jumped back
and blew a loud snort. The entrance to
the drain was no more than a small hole
now, but Sheltie knew that Emma was
inside.

He pawed at the ground frantically as

Emma's face appeared at the small
opening. The hole was large enough to
look through but far too small to crawl
out of. Emma didn't want to try and
move anything in case it made things
worse.

Instead, she looked to Sheltie for help.

'Go and fetch Dad, Sheltie,' she called.
'Fetch Dad! Quickly!'

Sheltie stood looking at Emma's face
peering out of the small hole in the pipe.
He cocked his head to one side,
listening.

'Go on,' urged Emma again. 'Fetch
help, Sheltie. Go and get Dad!'

Sheltie flicked his tail then turned and
galloped back through the woods as fast
as he could, kicking up piles of leaves.

Emma sat very still. She hugged

Scamp on her lap and waited. She was
too scared to move in case the drain
shifted again and collapsed on top of
her. Emma hoped it wouldn't be long
before Sheltie brought help.

Chapter Nine

Sheltie galloped all the way through the woods without stopping until he found someone who could help. But it wasn't Dad. It was Fred Berry out on one of his walks.

'Hello, Sheltie,' said Fred. 'What are you doing out here all on your own? Where's Emma?' He spoke gently as he took up the pony's reins.

Sheltie whinnied loudly and blew

puffs of steam into the cold air. Fred knew straight away that something was wrong. Sheltie was already pulling Fred along, urging him to hurry.

'Go on, then, Sheltie. Take me to Emma.'

Fred let go of the reins and Sheltie took off down the lane. Fred followed at a run and did his best to keep up. Before long he was huffing and puffing his way through the back wood and stumbling after Sheltie into the gully. The whole time he was calling out Emma's name.

'Emma! Emma!' His voice echoed through the trees. Emma heard him and yelled back.

'Over here. I'm in here! I'm trapped in a big pipe.'

Scamp heard Fred too and started

barking. Sheltie showed Fred the collapsed drain and when Fred saw it he gasped.

'Emma, are you all right?' he said.

'Yes, we're OK,' answered Emma.

'Whatever you do, don't make any sudden movements,' said Fred. He peered through the opening. 'Slide back slowly into the pipe and keep a tight hold of Scamp.'

Emma did as she was told and Fred started to pull at the concrete blocking the entrance.

The piece of drain which had collapsed was very heavy. It moved slightly but Fred wasn't quite strong enough to pull it free. He needed some help. But he didn't want to leave Emma alone and trapped inside.

Then Sheltie blew a really loud snort and nudged Fred gently in the small of his back. He seemed to be telling Fred that he could help.

Fred looked at Sheltie. Then he had an idea.

'If only I had a rope or something, Emma, then I could tie it to the broken pipe and get Sheltie to help me pull it free! But where will I find a rope?'

'There's a rope tied to Sheltie's saddle,' yelled Emma. 'And I've got a long lead in here too!' She crawled forward carefully and passed the long leather lead through the hole.

Fred tied the lead around the piece of pipe and looped the rope through it. He then fixed the rope to Sheltie's girth. Now there were two of them to pull.

'Ready, Sheltie?' said Fred.

Sheltie snorted and looked as though he was ready to pull. The little pony seemed to know exactly what he was expected to do.

Together, Fred and Sheltie pulled as hard as they could. The rope strained taut and suddenly the broken pipe fell

away as the rope pulled it free. Scamp
bounded out and Emma escaped
unhurt.

Sheltie did a little stomping dance
and pushed his soft muzzle into
Emma's tummy. Then he lowered his
head and licked Scamp's ears. Scamp
rolled over on to his back and wriggled
his legs in the air.

Fred told Emma that she should
never have crawled into the drainpipe.

'You should have gone for help,' he
said.

'But I couldn't leave Scamp,' pleaded
Emma. 'He was so scared.'

Scamp jumped up at Fred and licked
his hand. Fred smiled and said, 'Just
what is Emma going to do with you,
Scamp?'

Emma grinned. She understood now that they couldn't really keep Scamp at the cottage. The little dog could be quite a handful. He needed someone who could look after him all the time and train him properly. Someone who needed company as much as Scamp needed a home.

Then Emma had a brilliant idea!

Fred Berry was all alone in his cottage when Dad and Emma popped by that afternoon. They also had Sheltie and Scamp with them. Fred seemed very pleased to have visitors.

Emma told Fred all about what had happened when they had found Scamp's owner.

'. . . and we thought that if you liked

the idea, then you could have Scamp to keep for your very own!' she said.

The old man was overjoyed. Scamp had already taken an instant liking to Fred and was curled up at his feet in front of the fire.

'I think I like that idea very much, Emma,' said Fred. He had tears in his eyes as he spoke.

'No one could ever replace Jasper, but I'm sure Scamp and I will be very happy together. He's a smashing little fella.' Fred leaned forward and scratched Scamp's ears.

The little dog gave a sigh of contentment and fell fast asleep.

Emma took a photograph of Scamp and Fred.

'This will make a perfect ending for